W9-BHO-168

WITHDRAWN

Duck, Duck, Porcupine!

Salina Yoon

BLOOMSBURY
NEW YORK LONDON OXFORD NEW DELHI SYDNEY

For Lily and Tansy, with love!

Copyright © 2016 by Salina Yoon
All rights reserved. No part of this book may be reproduced or transmitted in any form or by any means, electronic or mechanical, including photocopying, recording, or by any information storage and retrieval system, without permission in writing from the publisher.

First published in the United States of America in May 2016
by Bloomsbury Children's Books
www.bloomsbury.com

Bloomsbury is a registered trademark of Bloomsbury Publishing Plc

For information about permission to reproduce selections from this book, write to Permissions, Bloomsbury Children's Books, 1385 Broadway, New York, New York 10018
Bloomsbury books may be purchased for business or promotional use. For information on bulk purchases please contact Macmillan Corporate and Premium Sales Department at specialmarkets@macmillan.com

Library of Congress Cataloging-in-Publication Data
Names: Yoon, Salina, author.
Title: Duck, Duck, Porcupine! / Salina Yoon.
Description: New York : Bloomsbury Children's Books, 2016.
Summary: Big Duck likes to boss around her younger brother, Little Duck, and she fancies herself the leader of their trio when joined by their gentle friend Porcupine. Little Duck does not speak yet, but through his expressions and his actions, he shows that he has a better grasp on any situation than his older sister.
Identifiers: LCCN 2015022813
ISBN 978-1-61963-723-8 (hardcover) • ISBN 978-1-61963-812-9 (e-book) • ISBN 978-1-61963-869-3 (e-PDF)
Subjects: | CYAC: Ducks—Fiction. | Brothers and sisters—Fiction. | Porcupines—Fiction. | BISAC: JUVENILE FICTION/Animals/Ducks, Geese, etc. | JUVENILE FICTION/Social Issues/Friendship. | JUVENILE FICTION/Family/Siblings.
Classification: LCC PZ7.Y817 Du 2016 | DDC [E]—dc23
LC record available at http://lccn.loc.gov/2015022813

Art created digitally using Adobe Photoshop
Typeset in Cronos Pro
Book design by Salina Yoon and Colleen Andrews
Printed in China by Leo Paper Products, Heshan, Guangdong
1 3 5 7 9 10 8 6 4 2

All papers used by Bloomsbury Publishing, Inc., are natural, recyclable products made from wood grown in well-managed forests. The manufacturing processes conform to the environmental regulations of the country of origin.

Three Short Stories

One

A Perfect Day for a Picnic

Two

I Think I Forgot Something!

Three

The Campout

One

A Perfect Day for a Picnic

This is a perfect day for a picnic, Porcupine!

Yes it is, Big Duck!

Little Duck and I will get the picnic basket.

I will get the picnic blanket.

We are all set!
Let's go!

Did you feel that?
Uh-oh!
plop!

munch
munch

Rain!
Our picnic is ruined!

plop!

Little Duck?!
slish-
slosh!

LITTLE DUCK!

SPLASH!

SPLISH
SPLASH

This is FUN!

TODAY is a perfect day for a picnic. The sun is out!
But there is no rain!

Two

I Think I Forgot Something!

I think I forgot something— but I can't remember what it is!

Maybe walking will work. Think, Big Duck, think!

I don't have time for presents, Little Duck. I am busy thinking!

For
Porcupine

Birthday
Party!

It is a big day—
but what is it?

Friday was flapping.
Saturday was napping.
What was Sunday?

You are invited!

I can't think when you are pecking, Little Duck!
tap!
tap!

peck!
peck!
CALE

Quack quack quack quack
QUACK-QUACK!

Why are you quacking "Happy Birthday"? It is not my birthday!

Where are you going, Little Duck?

For
Porcupine

WAIT!
I put this string on my finger to remind me of something.
For Porcupine

I've got it! It is . . .
Porcupine's birthday!
For Porcupine

Happy birthday, Porcupine!
For Porcupine

You remembered!
Porcupine

Of course I did!
How could I forget?

Three

The Campout

Let's go camping!

But I don't know how.

Do not worry, Porcupine.
Camping is easy!
I will make a list.

CAMPING LIST
1. tent
2. snacks
3. sleeping bags
4. flashlight
5. more snacks

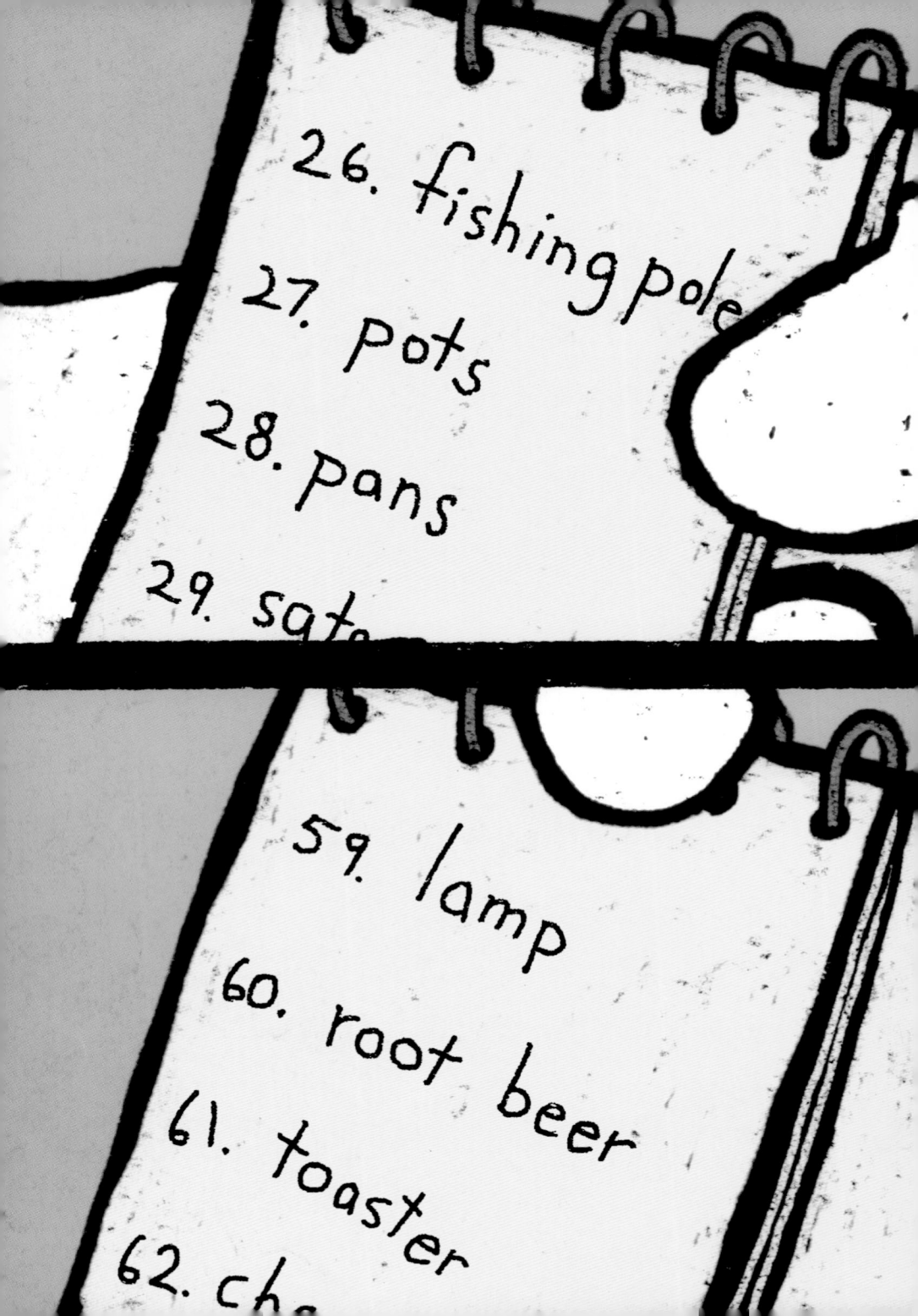
26. fishing pole
27. pots
28. pans
29. sat
59. lamp
60. root beer
61. toaster
62. ch

This is a long list, Big Duck!
You can't be too prepared, Porcupine!

Why do we need #78, the shovel?
In case of a snowstorm!

And #83, the blow-up raft?
In case of a flash flood! It is better to be safe than sorry.

Are we ready to go camping yet, Big Duck?

Not yet!

We are missing #99.
THE KITCHEN SINK?!
SNAC

MORE
SNACKS

I think we will need a truck.
I think I just want to go home.

crackle —
crackle —

Little Duck is CAMPING!
Of course he is, because he has item #100 . . .

crackle
crackle

. . . marshmallows!
I told you camping was easy!